LULU

AND THE CHOCOLATE WEDDING

FOR STEPHEN

Picture books by Posy Simmonds

FRED

LULU AND THE FLYING BABIES

BOUNCING BUFFALO

F-FREEZING ABC

LAVENDER

A RED FOX BOOK 0 09 945116 6

First published in Great Britain as *The Chocolate Wedding* by
Jonathan Cape, an imprint of Random House Children's Books

Jonathan Cape edition published 1990
Red Fox edition published 2003

1 3 5 7 9 10 8 6 4 2

Red Fox Books are published by Random House Children's Books,
61–63 Uxbridge Road, London W5 5SA; 20 Alfred Street, Milsons Point, Sydney,
NSW 2061, Australia; 18 Poland Road, Glenfield, Auckland 10, New Zealand; Endulini,
5A Jubilee Road, Parktown 2193, Johannesburg, South Africa

THE RANDOM HOUSE GROUP Limited Reg. No. 954009
www.kidsatrandomhouse.co.uk

A CIP catalogue record for this book is available from the British Library.

Printed in Hong Kong

LULU
AND THE CHOCOLATE WEDDING

POSY SIMMONDS

RED FOX

Lulu is going to be a bridesmaid in a silvery pink dress....

Her Aunt Carrie is going to be a bride in a long white one. *Everyone* at Lulu's school knows this.

Lulu will be staying at her grandparents' house for the wedding....

On the evening before the wedding, Lulu, her mother and father and her little brother, Willy, drive to Granny and Grandpa's house........

All the grown-ups are busy moving furniture and preparing food for the wedding party.....

Lulu and Willy go in the dining room. The wedding cake sits on a table covered in a long, white cloth. It looks much smaller today....not nearly as big as Mrs Clarke.

Lulu hides in a corner, near the radiator.

Inside her case are all the things she and Willy have been given for Easter: chocolate eggs, chocolate money, six chocolate soldiers and six chocolate kittens.....

Lulu eats three chocolate kittens and sixteen eggs.

Some of the eggs have insides she doesn't like.

Eeuch!

She spits these out.... and hides them under the radiator.

YUK!

Lulu always puts things she doesn't like behind radiators. There's already a bit of beetroot from supper...and a biscuit she got tired of.

Cake!

Man!

Lady!

Willy?   What you doing?

No!

Will-ee?

What you eating? ...show me!

No!

Elaahh!

Owh, **NO!**

There aren't enough beds for everyone at Granny's house. Lulu is sleeping on the sofa.....

It's the next day and everyone is ready to go to the church for the wedding, except Lulu. She was very sick in the night. She still feels ill.....

You keep nice and warm...and we'll be back very soon

Jenny from next door...

...and the ladies doing the waitressing will all keep an eye on you.

Lulu watches Aunt Carrie get into the wedding car. It's not a silver carriage. It's Grandpa's car, with white ribbons on it.

sniff!

There, Lulu...have a little snooze.....

BOO-HOO!

BOOo-HOOo!

?

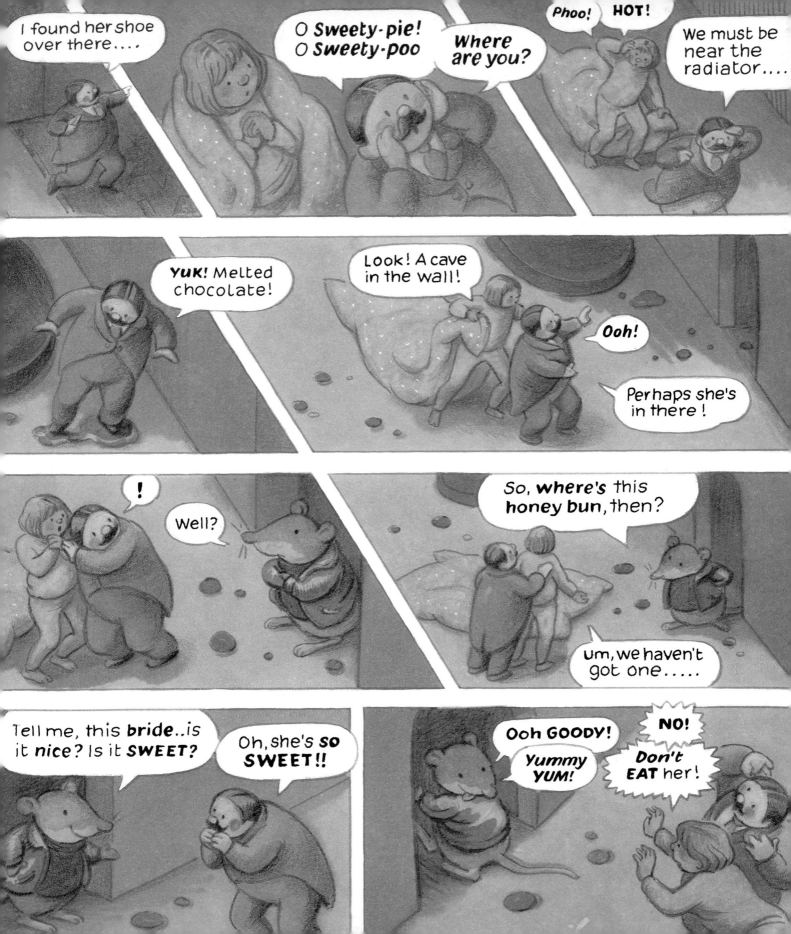

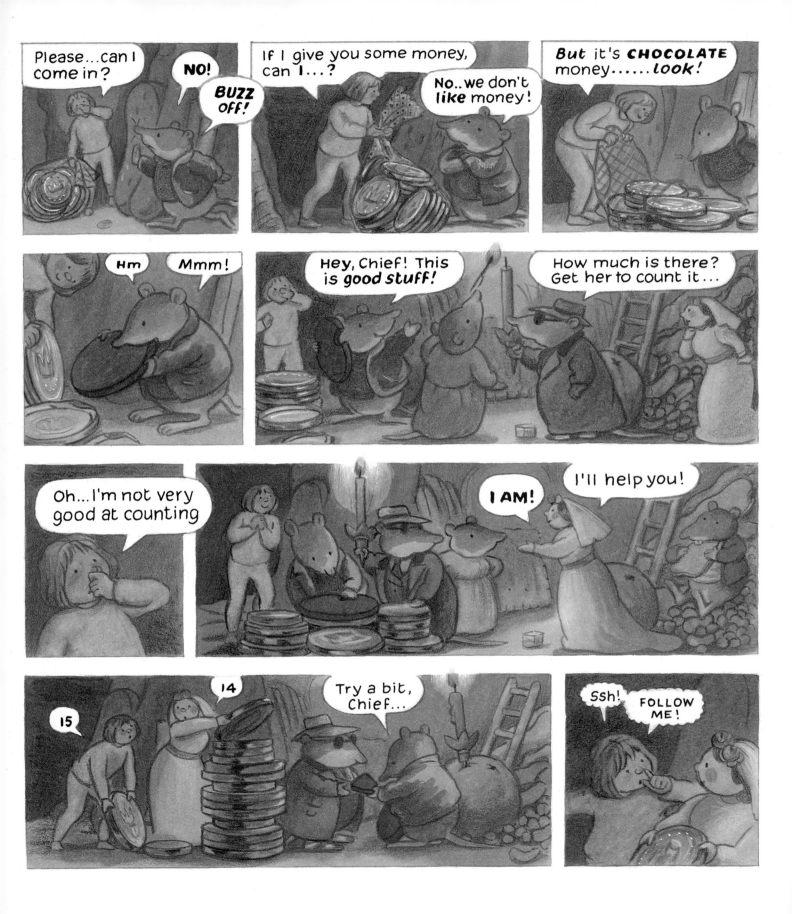

To Sweety-pie
and Sweety-poo!